Secret Thoughts Of A Common Man

H. G. Bramzel

Order this book online at www.trafford.com
or email orders@trafford.com

Most Trafford titles are also available at major online book retailers.

Printed in Victoria, BC, Canada.

ISBN: 978-1-4251-9038-5 (Soft)
ISBN: 978-1-4251-9040-8 (e-book)

*We at Trafford believe that it is the responsibility of us all, as both individuals
and corporations, to make choices that are environmentally and socially sound.
You, in turn, are supporting this responsible conduct each time you purchase a
Trafford book, or make use of our publishing services. To find out how you are
helping, please visit www.trafford.com/responsiblepublishing.html*

*Our mission is to efficiently provide the world's finest, most comprehensive
book publishing service, enabling every author to experience success.
To find out how to publish your book, your way, and have it available
worldwide, visit us online at www.trafford.com*

Trafford rev. 11/05/2009

Trafford
PUBLISHING®   www.trafford.com

North America & international
toll-free: 1 888 232 4444 (USA & Canada)
phone: 250 383 6864 ♦ fax: 812 355 4082 ♦ email: info@trafford.com

BSD

Dedicated to all those who have touched my life...
                                    ... and I theirs...

Through the intellect man distinguishes between the true and the false...
... not "good and evil"...
(Maimonides, 1135-1204, Guide For The Perplexed)

The Author

CREDITS

Cover photo: shutterstock, Design: www.simmel-artwork.de
Contact the author: secretthoughts@ymail.com

THE AUTHOR

Harvey G. Bramzel, known in Israel as Zvi Bar, was born in London, England on 14th March 1950, in the very same hospital where he would later train, The London Hospital, Whitechapel. His sister followed him into this world four and a half years later. His family left the East End of London for Aveley, Essex. There he spent the next couple of years of early childhood while his parents tried to overcome their regret at leaving the capital. When that regret could not be assuaged they moved back to Greater London. The latter part of his childhood was spent in Burnt Oak, Edgware, in the County of Middlesex.

Being of a scientific bent and influenced, perhaps, by his father's sad attempts to come to terms with diabetes, he decided to study medicine. He earned his degree at The London Hospital in 1973 and went on to practice as a family physician until 1976. In that year he decided to embark on another path in life and come to Israel. Venturing on various paths has been a characteristic of his throughout and one that he has never regretted.

In Israel he specialized in Anesthesiology and over the next 30 years became deputy head of department in one of Israel's main government hospitals, Tel Hashomer, and Chief of Anesthesia in Assuta, Israel's largest private hospital.
He has written papers on various subjects in anesthesiology but felt that he needed to express himself in other directions.
His family life has been turbulent, signposted with difficult relationships but blessed with five wonderful children.

At the age of 56 he turned to writing poetry. It was not a matter of choice so much as an inordinate compulsion to express thoughts and feelings that had matured over time and been subjected to vivid experience. It is these he wishes to share with you in the hope that his attempts in translating personal experience and sentiment into a more universally empathetic composition will succeed in sounding a personal chord in his readers.

CONTENTS

BITTERSWEET

ROMANTIC

ROMANTIC (contd.)

SAD

PHILOSOPHICAL

PHILOSOPHICAL (contd.)

WHIMSICAL

BITTERSWEET

A FLAT TIRE ON THE HIGHWAY OF LOVE

Onward sped that sleek machine.
In playful joy devoured the miles,
while trees flashed by as in a dream,
accelerating fields and stiles,
despite my tongue-in-cheek denials.

The scenic route stole breath away,
the wind tugged playfully at our hair.
With you alone, a perfect day!
The road stretched like the Milky Way.
We rode the breeze without a care.

From out of sun-soaked balmy skies,
with no prior warning where or whence,
a tire's scream, its piercing cries
jarred our softly intoned sighs
as we stopped by a rustic fence.

A wheel was shred beyond repair.
The perfect day in an instant fled.
The wind still tugged at our unkempt hair
but the easy mood changed to despair
with romantic thoughts still left unsaid.

Would we together change that wheel
or has the wind now veered its tack?
Would we together face life's ordeal,
or would you pout devoid of zeal
while I get out the spare and jack?

Love's journey winds a tricky road,
long stretches pass without a hitch.
The truest test if you'll bear the load
is not in times when fortune flowed
but now when tossed into a ditch.

A GILDED CAGE

A mockingbird once flew to me
and prayed to let it stay.
It begged me not to set it free
for ever and a day.

I've naught to give but a gilded cage
to house your nature wild.
Like a learn'ed book without bound page,
or rich but orphaned child.

At last its pleas, my need,
indeed, together did conspire.
So though in doubt, I did consent
to warm it by my fire.

All winter long it joyed my heart.
The cage door left ajar,
its choice alone to stay with me,
or go and fly afar.

The ice-bound months of winter passed.
Balding snow exposed the flowers.
Exuberant sounds of spring at last
began to fill our sun-starved hours.

My mockingbird awoke anew
to summer's call, its vows forgot.
The scent of roses tipped with dew
enticed to slip the love-tied knot.

The gilded cage once more lies bare,
the hearth, cold ash of winter's fire.
The creaking call of the cage's door
a sad refrain for my heart's desire.

BEFORE YOU GO

Kiss me softly before you go.
Take my hand that I may know
that sweet memories will outlast the tears
and reckless words not spoil the years.
That even though I hurt you so,
and thus our love has ceased to grow,
the warmth and friendship that we knew,
that in adversity saw us through,
will not in anger be denied.
At least to make amends we tried.
Hold me once before you go.
Stroke my cheek that I may know,
that even though our ways must part,
I'll not be banished from your heart.

CYCLE OF LOVE

My Love is but an autumn leaf
fallen from a bough.
And once where luscious green was seen,
crisp browns adorn it now.

'Twas parting leaf in season made
by Nature's fixed decree,
but was the timing of it's fall
in part because of me?

Once winter's passed, the snow is gone,
spring's vital force returns,
and I will see new leaves of green
for which my nature yearns.

Still, I know that seasons pass
and joy makes way for sorrow.
The pain forgotten once again
must needs return tomorrow.

Thus in endless cycle turn
the greens to browns and fade,
to be reborn, the phoenix fire
turning burnished gold to jade.

DON'T TELL ME THAT YOU LOVE ME

Don't tell me that you love me,
just show me that you care.
I don't need your arms about me
when you don't know how to share.

Love can be demonstrated,
but that's not what I need.
True love is not outdated
though ambition takes the lead.

If you really mean it,
as you forcefully declare,
that you'll be mine forever
then make sure you're really there.

For I would rather be without an intermittent love
that's sometimes there, sometimes in doubt,
a fickle love that only knows
when to shun and when to pose.

I COVERED YOU WITH KISSES

I covered you with kisses
and gently took your hand.
Together we left imprints
on a warm and distant land.

Your heart was mine forever,
to you I gave my soul.
Forever and together
each part greater than the whole.

But nothing lasts eternal,
even memories have faded.
The love that was its kernel
to dust crumbled, fervor jaded.

Our tears once mixed in laughter,
now each drop falls alone
to mourn for ever after
the love you have outgrown.

I smothered you with kisses
and led you by the hand,
but now am left in sorrow
in a stark and distant land.

IN LOVE WITH THE WOMAN YOU WERE

Yes, I am still in love with the woman I thought you were.
I am, and always will be, resentful of the cruel effigy
that has usurped her place.

As a drawn illusion compels my mind to see a shape and then,
in an instant, the image is gone to be replaced by another.
The same lines on the page, a different image in my thoughts.
So have you become, my love.

You ask, "How can you love me one minute and shun me the next?"
And I reply, "I am so in love with the woman I lost
and flee from that other who has taken her place".
Like the illusion, each of you has the same lines,
but the image in my heart is different.

Where is my love that spoke of the swans who pair for life?
Is she somehow imprisoned inside the shell of this cruelly hard
and calculating effigy?
Was she present, silenced within that form
that so cynically slew the swans?
Did she cry for help within that shell?
Bang with her fists on the casing of her soul,
and was I deaf?

Or is the illusion just in my mind?

Yes, my actions are erratic.
I am both cruel and kind to this image that claims to be my love.
I pine for the one I have lost,
and abhor the one that has inherited her body.

Where are you, my love?
Or were you ever there at all...?

LOVE BIRD

My love is like a timid bird
and in its nest,
at my behest,
it lays its fragile word.

Faith, hope and mostly trust
at mercy to abuse and lust.
Within love's nest each fragile shell
rests in place just where it fell.

So easy to break, those wafer shells,
a tap, a crack,
an unresponsive back,
each sordid act retells.

And once its surface has been cracked,
like a city that's been sacked,
what lies within will surely die
with barely a whimper
or stifled sigh.

LOVE'S QUEST

Be not sad for me
if I have loved in vain.
See not my dried-up tears,
feel not my heart-wrenched pain.

Willing I trod the path
that often spawns despair
and many places have I been,
fond memories still dwell there.

A lover's heart is forged in pain,
true love is but a mist.
But ever onward are we drawn
by promise of a kiss.

And if by some enchanted fate
my heart's desire I'll one day meet,
all previous hurt would melt away
as ice devoured in passion's heat.

MY LIFE, AN EMPTY SHELL

I have wept so many tears
the sea cries out, "no more!
If those nimbus eyes of yours don't dry
I'll overrun the shore."

So many nights I've lain awake
yearning for your touch,
the morning sun no longer tries
to warm me very much.

The birds and flowers, romantic nymphs,
that once assumed their role
and charmed our days of joyous love
take pity on my soul.

So Nature too can try no more
now that your magic's gone,
and I am left an empty shell,
my features drawn and wan.

MY SHIP OF GLASS

Like a ship of glass
on leaden waves
my fragile heart
your softness craves.
But my senses perched
high on the mast
detect a storm
approaching fast.

I fear her sailors
will all be lost.
Naught but your eyes
will count the cost
as beneath those waves
her cargo slips.
O Love that's sunk
a thousand ships!

ODE TO LOVE LOST

Spread your soft caress
on my fevered brow
and whisper fond endearments
in my imploring ear.
Let my dried-out lips once more
brush against your sweet moist skin.
Breathe back life into my soul
and make me live again.

Light these faded eyes
with the passion of your fire,
and with the bellows of your spirit
rekindle embers of desire.
Unlock the secret chambers of my heart,
whose only key lies in your hand,
and walk with me once more
where the salty sea
smoothes discord from the sand.

Hold my limp and lifeless hand in yours
as we stroll along the shore
and by rolling waves, insistent breeze,
make me believe we will remain
as one for evermore.

PACKING UP OUR LIFE

The removal men came.
Veni, vidi, vici!

They swaggered into our life,
uninvited by me but,
with my polite, restrained acquiescence,
violating our shared intimacy,
exposing the nude, bruised body of our love.

You ministered over the dissection
of our togetherness,
while I sat on the balcony
nonchalantly solving sudoku puzzles
and reading current affairs,
all the while seeing my own emotional disorder
in multi-faceted reflection
off the pages of the news magazine.

I remember well how they turned up the radio,
the tinny pop percolating throughout the house
and reverberating in the solitary halls
of my mind.

Sweat-provoking labor
demands a convalescent pause.
They used it to invade
the bastion of my solitude.
They clouded the pretence of my aloofness
with cigarette smoke and idle banter.
"Lived here long?" enquired their leader,
lounging in my chaise longue,
his approving eye trespassing the view
our intimacy alone had owned.

I mumbled incoherently,
without raising a glance from my industry,
as if partaking in those affairs
my eyes were reading of
but which were, in fact,
decoupled from my thoughts.

How easy it is to pack up the props
that embellished the tragic conclusion to our co-existence.
But their ghosts remain
long after the hired assassins received their reward and moved on.
They haunt the silent spaces
where our laughter once echoed
and mock the stillborn aspirations
of our stilted love.

SHIPWRECKED

Forsaken on a barren shore,
all pretense left behind,
to never see you anymore,
to wipe you from my mind.

We used to bathe in azure waves
beneath such balmy skies,
but love-seared nights and friendship days
were innocence or lies.

If I had known you then, My Love,
as now you are revealed,
I'd not have seen the stars above
nor parted lips once sealed.

But now the footsteps in the sand
are deep and mine alone.
The heart that took you by the hand
has naivety outgrown.

O that I'd not sailed that reef
that overturned our craft,
or been exposed to lover's grief
by Cupid's misaimed shaft.

For what is joy that ends in pain,
the latter to endure
far longer than the love we gain,
for which there is no cure?

Would we rather love and lose
than never love at all?
And were we ever asked to choose
when passion paid its call?

But now alone on shingled shore,
my thoughts in disarray,
all hope of rescue I ignore,
no beacon lights my way.

And yet, I know that I'll survive
to leave this lonely beach.
In time my senses will revive,
my heart another's reach.

THE JASMINE IS IN BLOOM AGAIN

The jasmine has bloomed again.
You remember how, when we bought it
and brought it home,
we discovered a pest feasting off its luscious leaves?

We were so in love
and I oblivious to the frustration
that nibbled at your soul.

I bought a spray for the jasmine
and you treated it.
You were the one with green fingers.

If only the fingers of my insight had been as green
to caress away your torment.

The jasmine seemed to recover
but refused to flower again.

Bye and bye, you decided that,
if you were to heal yourself
then we must part.

My life drained of its tinted hues.
The subtly cool-shaded greens of our garden
could no longer calm my festering spirit.
I needed an invigorating distraction of color
and planted riotous hues of begonia.
You saw them that day,
before you left.

The seasons have moved on.
You tell me that
you love me still
and would return,
you with the healing green fingers.

As if sensing their impending redundancy,
the begonias have died.
Hasten back! The jasmine is flowering once more.

THE OLD HOUSE

Hello Old Friend! It's strange beyond ken
to see your bougainvillea smile again.
It's been a while,
I see it in your faded tile
and peeling paint around your eyes.
Like me, appearance tells no lies.
Do laughter and tears still echo in your beams,
like me, do memories return as dreams,
or are your thoughts now occupied
with others that now live inside?

By chance I happened down this street,
or, perhaps, your siren call did guide my feet.
Does your memory of brick and stone
recall one whose light went out as surely as your own?
But whereas yours in an instant returns,
for hers my heart eternal yearns.
Farewell O Friend, whose mortar and stone,
with apathy, memories so readily disown.
If only I could be like you,
forget sad thoughts and start anew!

THE PRICE OF OUR LOVE

I look into your sapphire eyes
and see the embers of the fire
I once ignited.
I lie next to you,
a log forsaken in the forest of abandoned dreams.
In our former existence
my very presence in your bed
excited you.
Now it is a threat.
The centimeters that separate us
are centuries, light years.
Once I could have died for your touch
Now I die without it.
I would prefer our love to burn in
an explosion of passionate discord
than in this false, plastic imitation
of mutual politeness and political correction.
I hurt therefore I am,
and, in being, suffer the torment of loving you.
Such is the price of love…

TORTURED LOVE

Cruel, deformed, impervious love!
Your alchemy of nonchalant neglect
has transmuted my erstwhile doting heart
from a fervent, pure spirit
into a mechanical, rusting, spare part.

The sweet waters of tearful joy
in which we once bathed
have turned bitter with resent.
No more warmth could I engender,
with no endearment force your relent.

But so it is with beauty tarnished.
If an orchid bent by a gust of wind
could be straightened once more or underpinned
would it be fresh as new,
or a gross effigy of what once was true?

Better by far memories fond
of adolescent yearning and stolen glance,
when from the world shut away in trance
our love pirouetted
in intoxicating dance.

TURMOIL!

My mind is in such turmoil,
dark thoughts pursue their tails.
I try to concentrate ideas
which race along like snails.

What once was calm and order
no longer seems that way.
Like socks of different colors
my thoughts in disarray.

You told me that you'd love me
for "ever and a day."
I'd be content with "ever",
but now you've gone away.

You still claim that you love me
but that it's best apart.
You left with little warning
and took my broken heart.

At least, I hope it is with you
for I feel it's no more here.
But if it's lost you'll doubtless shed
a crocodile-like tear.

You say for you it's difficult
and I don't understand.
But when we loved you claimed I was
the wisest in the land.

My mind remains in turmoil,
my thoughts in disarray.
If only I could understand
such love that turns away!

UNDER A LEAFY MAPLE TREE

I loved My Love.
My Love loved me
under a leafy maple tree.

Her skin so fair,
my heart so true,
our hands entwined in morning dew.

We pledged our love
and made our vows
as the breeze blew warmly thru' its boughs.

But then a word spoke out of place,
a harsh reply from a fallen face.
A new resolve from a hardened will.
The branches trembled in evening chill.

I lost My Love.
My Love left me
under a leafy maple tree.

UNREQUITED LOVE

I dive into your stormy eyes,
my senses drown, your ocean sighs
my name... and I am lost.
I feel no danger, count no cost.

To save me would be so in vain
for I would plunge again, again,
forever striving with desire,
a moth incinerated in your fire.

A love like mine is doomed to drink
the hemlock of a poet's ink
and tortured dreams be laid to rest,
by Cupid's arrow fired in jest.

WILD RED ROSE

O sweet, wild flower,
O heart-red rose!
Among your thorns
such beauty flows!

Such caring love
and warm embrace.
My senses drown
in your perfumed grace.

From my tired eyes
you banish sleep,
my restless spirit
in torment keep.

O that to grasp you
I would dare
to possess such delicate
beauty rare!

But with your love
I'd too feel pain,
your thorns with blood
the petals stain.

And dew-shaped tears
would I then shed
for love abused
and thoughts unsaid.

ROMANTIC

A BLANK PAGE

I sit at my desk, pen in hand,
and let my thoughts freely expand
to fill the universe of joy and pain,
to feel, to taste, and yes, to tame
emotions borne of trial and age
upon a never-ending page.

Its pristine unfathomable white
can serve as backdrop for the night
of nefarious deeds or betrayed love,
as well as day of chansoned cheer
to chase away that night-filled tear.

It lays upon my desk
pregnant with desire,
awaiting impatiently my pen's caress,
for secret thoughts to lustily undress.
To satisfy the reason for its birth,
for its creation on an earth
where wondrous intricate tales unfold,
each jostling expression to be told,
and once its ardor has been spent,
to return again from whence was sent.

But will this wanton siren sheet,
whose fallow lines horizons meet,
be satisfied or disappointed shrink
from the dark-stained thoughts
of lascivious ink?
Will its textured face smile
on a lover's gentle touch
giving so little though promising so much?

Or would it remain pristine,
a virgin page, innate beauty unseen,
until by virtue of words more skilled
its arcane desire be at last fulfilled?

A LOVER'S WISH

Her body clothed in velvet night,
the contours of her breath I sought,
as in her soft repose she stirred.
Such beauty in frail moonlight wrought!

Her slumber sung in lilting sighs,
no doubt she dreamed, perchance of me,
and I, a sentry, stood on watch
over gentle form, her slave would be.

If she should wake before the dawn
I would her wine-red lips implore
to calm my fevered soul in kiss
as she had oft bestowed before.

And if 'tis I who fall asleep
before she wakes, O grant me this,
that she take pity on my love
and consummate my dream with bliss!

A WINTER STROLL

Emerald fingers caress my brow
as liquefying crystals' wordless speech
confer wintry thoughts
to dampened cheeks,
their meaning clear but out of reach,

Silken caresses tug my hair
while chapped lips shape soundless prose.
A lullaby of moaning wind,
memoriam to lily fair and scented rose,
rock stark trees in frost repose.

Feathers soft on stony soil,
shapeless ghosts of seasons died,
twigs brittle swaying to-and-fro
the fertility of their bounty hide,
as if unable to decide.

Sunken steps in progress slow
along the hidden paths I wind,
Shivery mist from exhaled breath,
their form like a memory in my mind,
draw wispy contrails undefined.

AN APPARITION OF BEAUTY

She was an apparition,
hidden from the light that shines on most men
and illuminates their coarse features.

Hers was a light that glowed from within,
that suffused her being with a soft and mellow beauty.

My raging heart longed to extinguish its fire
in the cool calm of her waters.
And yet, to possess her was to destroy her.

Like red-hot iron plunged into a sacred stream,
the profane thrust into the holy.
The iron neither remaining red-hot nor the waters cool and calm.
Thus lust extinguishes romance.

The iridescence of the mayfly's wing,
so beautiful, so ephemeral,
is gone.
So too the mayfly.

All that remains,
a lump of iron in a muddy stream.

And yet, before my frailty steals the memory away,
I see her still.
An apparition of beauty,
glowing from within.

AUTUMN

falling gently through the branches,
ever downward never pausing,
twirling madly dervish dances,
golden speckled brownly coursing,
discarded memories of sun
baring nests now deserted,
exposing wizened bone,
naked branches all alone,
waiting, wanting, for a smile,
hoping, yearning all the while
for sign of gilded orb anew
to clothe with green, anoint with dew.

COME, WALK WITH ME

Your voice sighs softly in my ear,
sweet lips brush mine your breath so near.
I draw you in, within my soul,
what once I lacked your love makes whole.
If I could lose myself in bliss,
immersed, enveloped in your kiss,
to give, to take, to share and find
within warm beauty and sweet mind,
a kindred spirit, soft of grace,
grievous fortune would I face.
My only wish would ever be
to hold your hand, come, walk with me.

ENSLAVED BY LOVE

I stand defenseless
before the onslaught of your beauty.
Paralyzed in awe of your presence
and humbled by my need in your absence.

You are everything I have ever desired
even though I was oblivious of those desires.
I have awakened to a slavery
that has liberated me from all others.

If you have imperfections I cherish them,
for they are the individual flaws
that make an artist's work unique.
The counterpoint setting of a precious jewel.

To draw the fire of your untamed love
I would expose my innermost self.
To retain it I would give my being,
knowing that you would never abuse it.

It is within my desire to give all
and your forbearance not to demand it,
within that fulfillment of spiritual passion,
that true love abides.

HEADIER THAN WINE

Your silken hand so smoothes my brow,
your plush and luscious lips brush mine,
a glimpse of heaven, revealed now,
your presence headier than wine.

If I could choose to die in bliss,
this cold, harsh world to leave behind,
I'd choose your sweet departing kiss
to draw the curtains of my mind.

But if in charity you turn
to save so mortal one as I
then look with favored, sweet concern
in knowing and discerning eye.

For I have loved you from the first,
your sweetness captivates my heart.
You calm my hunger, quench my thirst,
to fevered thoughts such peace impart.

So take my trembling hand in yours
and guide me in your gentle way,
but ever often stop and pause,
my fears and sadness to allay.

JE T'ADORE

The sun's brazen glory cannot outshine
the beauty of your smile divine,
and the softest clouds in heaven's vault
against your silken skin are naught.

Your vermilion lips set hearts aflame
making the reddest rose blush with shame
and eyes that are pools of molten fire
envelope me in unquenched desire.

If I could but kiss your dulcet lips,
trace contours of your sculpted hips…
O if pouting breast of firm design
you would bequeath and make it mine!

If you would lend your heart to my soul's plea
I'd pledge to you my spirit free
and make a prisoner of my heart
to never live from you apart.
I'd serve and love you, je t'adore
from now until forever more!

LIKE A METEOR

Love, you soar like a meteor
through the night-chilled sky.
The moon pales with modesty in your blazing eye.
And in the splendor of your wake,
fleetingly, the heavens quake.
Venus, if in presence dare,
cannot return your piercing stare.
And Sirius, who at the moon would bay,
must avert his gaze and turn away.
And lo! no sooner have we sung your praise
the cool night air has quenched your blaze.

But those celestial gems of greater worth
persist, embed in Mother Earth.
They pulverize and vaporize,
destroy all in their path,
as if the might of heaven
has loosed his awful wrath.
But the land they change forever,
it will never be the same.
Even though this rock be buried
it denies not that it came.
And within its core of iron
it oft times does contain
the seeds of life, the residue,
of cosmic joy and pain.

LOVE WITHOUT END

If I could dream only of you
then I would sleep the whole day through
and cover your lily-fair skin in bliss
with kiss after kiss after tender kiss.

And if I should wake up by your side,
then would I hold you in love and pride
that so pretty a maid with heart so true
would stay with me the whole night through.

Oh, that such nights and days could last
and from the Present heal the Past
'till the Future, and from there extend,
Love all-encompassing, love without end.

NOT JUST YOUR TOUCH...

Not just the sparkling sapphire
of your understanding eyes,
nor the soft enticement
of your inviting thighs.
Neither soft-toned caresses
in love so tender voiced,
nor your gossamer, dreamlike touch
that leave my eyes so moist.
It is your soul I glimpsed
when last you held me to your heart.
It was your purity of spirit
that bids me ne'er depart.

O JERUSALEM!

Step-smoothed stones,
osteoporotic bones
supporting gold-domed splendor
which in modesty hides
dust-coated alleys
where poverty abides
with myrrh and frankincense,
furtive glances, shadows tense.

Long beards and veils together flow
through jostling souks and arches low.
Passing merchants' outstretched hands,
imploring gestures, festooned stands,
by twisting ways where urchins run
under awnings' sifted sun
to emerge in sudden glare
where cloistered courtyards pray and stare.

Bells and chants and muezzins' cry
in heavenward union chastely fly,
while supplicants on bended knee
form rippling waves on a prayerful sea.
And towering above the ancient gate,
in solitary and patient wait,
a sentinel of foregone might,
The Citadel commands the night.

ODE TO PASSION

Such passion lies between soft thighs
of beauty's earthly form.
Her blossomed lips and sculpted hips
my hungry eyes adorn.
For sweet caress of rose-bud breast
O I would gladly die,
to be reborn in misted dawn
with love's departing sigh.

THE MEMORY OF LOVE

A lasting gift you can bestow
is not the gift of love.
For love can be granted one fine day
and then, the next, is taken away.
The only thing that will remain,
after flow of joy and ebb of pain,
is the memory of love.

For while all else,
the impatient nervous wait
by a lonely secret gate,
the fiery furnace of desire
that makes our nonchalance a liar,
all these pass like a bubbling stream.
But the memory of love remains,
forever, a sweet recurring dream.

THOUGHTS

Where the sea meets the sky
there dwell I.
Seek me, if you will,
in the salty still
of wind-spent waves
and chill-dark foamy caves.
In the whispering breeze
like a lover's tease,
soft, almost intangible, touch,
hardly felt yet promising much.
Know me in the quiet chasms of your thought,
where much is seen, but little sought.
For in the cellars of your mind,
where in the darkness all are blind,
know the path you must pursue,
and that this quiet voice is you.

TRUE LOVE

You declare that you love me
and ask for my trust.
But is it really love you mean
or is it simply lust?

For lust is such a selfish love,
self-gratifies and heeds
only the insistent carnal call
of pleasure's basic needs.

Yes, you can pay for acquiescence
with a tender-voiced caress,
with kind words, flowers, presents,
for fulfilling your behest.

But for me 'tis only payment,
at the very best,
and, at worst, an off-hand gesture
of true sentiment divest.

The kind of love I need
lets budding flowers grow.
Sentiment reaps only fruits
a caring hand can sow.

So if you show you love me
with affection plainly shared,
we'll conquer such adversity
as most have never dared.

WHAT IS LOVE?

To feel that I am less than whole
when I am without you.
And far more than I ever dreamt I could be
when I am with you.

To love your body more than
I could ever love my own
and feel your emotion in my soul.
To let my joy soothe your sadness
and your smile make my spirit soar.

It is knowing that you feel
how much I love you
and need my love as much as I need yours.
To want you for ever
and to feel both safe in your love
and ever mindful of showing you mine.

WHITE DOVE

Soft, white dove on soaring wing
above the strife of serf and king.
Passion's pulse begins anew
moistened sweetly by love's dew.

Now the slumbering phoenix wakes
in covetous lust its thirst it slakes,
to be consumed by dire desire
in the thrust of passion's fire.

To live, to feel again the pains
of want and need in mortal veins!
To be transformed in thought and deed
and in embrace to sow life's seed.

Intoxicating, musky scent
envelops fields of passions spent.
While the phoenix now ashen lies
my white dove soars in azure skies.

YOU OPEN LIKE A FLOWER

You open like a flower.
Each tear-drop petal formed in sorrow
or in joy.
I close my eyes in bliss,
borne aloft on the heady fragrance
of your nascent sexuality.

SAD

A FATHER'S LAMENT

I watched him playing with his toys,
the warrior games of growing boys,
plastic guns and cardboard tanks,
the plots, the plans, the childhood pranks.

I saw him dress up with his friends,
the thrill of danger when death pretends.
Cowboys, soldiers, swords and shields,
the glamour of valor in Elysian fields.

And when he grew and I grew old
it was my joy to him behold.
A fine young man of steadfast eye
whose mature stature did youth belie.

Career and marriage, a future bright,
my glowing beacon in aged night.
A swell of pride in faltering step
to lend some strength to a hand inept.

But horizons dim with the nimbus of war
and we are distanced from decision's shore.
When wisdom flees before brute force
nefarious deeds sadly change life's course.

It is the bright of eye and springing gait
we send, while in trepidation wait.
The naïve and nurtured orchid rare
sent to places far and danger dare.

We follow in our hearts afar,
while salt-stained tears our visions mar.
Both proud and filled with morbid fear,
O would we be there and they be here!

If vengeful hate should mark him down
with remorseless fate for hallowed ground
would I, without a second thought,
take his place in danger fraught.

But destiny intention scorns
when a father his own son mourns.
Is there a greater pain than this,
with cold white cheek and tear-stained kiss?

DR. ALZHEIMER, I PRESUME...

When I'm not me who will I be?
Will you recognize me by my clothes
or by the room in which I dwell,
my very own body a prison cell
that once was me?
Will you my virtual self abhor,
edging ever closer to the door,
when you come to visit me?

But in comfort small you can partake
by considering me a fake
of him that you once knew.
Yes, we do look the same
although I can't recall my name.
But he that sat here once before
'twas he you really did adore
for his casual remarks made so witty,
whereas, now this earthly shell that's left
evokes your sadness and your pity.

And yet, from time to time,
while a spark of that old fire still burns,
the me you once knew returns,
briefly, to visit you.
And when you know I'm really here
to wipe away that salty tear
you also know that when I'm through
I'll be gone once more,
bidding you adieu,
to return from whence I came.
Do you still recognize me,
though I'm not the same...?

GRAVE ROBBERS

Ghosts of silent bells.
Freshly turned soil balefully mourning
its disruption.
Senses clogged with the smell
of damp clay.
Whispered words, devoid of comfort.
Terse instructions guiding the shovel.

The moon's sorrowful connivance
as it peeps furtively
from behind wispy lace.
A cough, a curse, a cuff, a cry,
but not from the sodden bowels of clod
which bear their rape in silent accusation.

Moan of the wind,
rustle of leaves dry as skin,
chorus in counterpoint.
Extinguished candle, impotent sentry.
Bark of distant dog.
Hoot of disdaining owl.

Scrape of iron on earth.
Tap of metal on wood,
its careful artistry exposed
to rough unloving hands.
Protesting groan as timbers yield
to a crowbar's brutal persuasion.
Pale flesh revealed in satin repose
impatiently torn from eternity
by calloused greed
to serve once more
the needs of lesser men.

REFLECTIONS ON YOUTH

Where are they now,
those sonnets on Love Divine?
Still on a dusty bookshelf,
they speak of flowers and wine.

And where are they, those sprite young men,
who fought a duel at dawn?
The one lies face down in dirt?
for both she must now mourn.

And she of radiant beauty fresh
whose face turned hearts and minds,
does she still remember youth
when faded picture finds?

O that our youth and memories
would stay forever new,
and that we could preserve from fate
evaporating dew!

For all once dear and grasped with pain
is wrench'ed from our hand,
and only man's impermanence
is written in life's sand.

SORROW

I am a whisper,
an unfinished thought,
the splash of a tear,
a sharp gasp of a slammed door,
the finality of fate,
the infinite sadness of silence
that drowns childhood's laughter,
I am...

THE BALLAD OF FLO'

Come gather ye round m' hearty lads
and hear me tell of Flo'
for there's nowt that cheers such wanton ears
as another's tale of woe.

Poor Flo' was born a maid forlorn
who loved her master so,
but he cast her out with a cruel clout,
alone with her babe in tow.

'Twas winter and the snow lay thick
upon the roads across the moors.
Not one kind face nor act of grace
to open shuttered doors.

And bye and bye the babe did die.
Its frozen corpse, a bundle small,
under a hedgerow made to lie.
Its innocent, accusing eye damning her and us withal.

Oh spiteful fate come early or late
its victims must enthrall.
None can escape such joy or hate
that needs us to befall.

We can but cheer and drink our beer
as closest to the fire
we warm our thoughts and heat our corpse
and plan to our heart's desire.

THE LONELY MAN

It was at a poetry reading that I met The Lonely Man.
He had arrived early, as had I.
His aged peaked cap and weathered nose intruded
self-consciously into the aroma of the coffee shop.
Wearing his beard like a muffler against the cold of despair,
he approached our table,
drawn in, like a primeval cosmic body at the birth of the universe,
forming a nucleus of human contact
amidst the cold interstellar background
of a late Tel Aviv evening.

I offered him my hand,
like throwing a lifebuoy to a drowning man.
He shook it limply,
implying that he had long ago resigned himself
to the fate of a castaway.
Perhaps comfortable in his watery milieu,
a solitary dolphin,
attracted by the lighted ships that pass in the night.
Drawn by curiosity, but anchored to familiarity.

"Do you write?" I ventured lamely.
"Oh no," he replied with infinite sadness,
"I don't know how to express myself in words."
"And yet there is something of the artist about you…" I continued
in a desperate attempt to resuscitate our ebbing contact.
"I draw…," he replied, as if my attempt at verbal first aid
had been answered by the first spontaneous intake of breath.
"Would you like to see?"

(contd.)

(contd.)

The Lonely Man had been pulled back
from the brink of conversational extinction.
In an exuberance of joyful reanimation he pulled a digital camera
from the deep recesses of his billowing jacket.
"I drew this in crayon while on a train journey in The States".
The illuminated screen was thrust before me as proof
that The Lonely Man had another existence, an alternate universe.

The scene depicted glowed in vivid childlike hues.
An impossibly azure sky crowned a verdant pasture
on which stood a group of people forming a circle.
The pasture was bisected by a river
the same color as the sky, flowing from a distant mountain.
On the far bank of the river stood a house,
and beached next to the house was a small boat.

"Do you notice anything special about the house?" enquired
The Lonely Man.
"It only has two windows," I replied hesitantly,
seeking approval of my acuity.
"And no doors!" he added jubilantly.
"That's my house. I have no doors, I can't get out!"
"And," my subconscious added, "no one else can get in..."
He scrolled the view to focus on the circle of figures.
"That's me," he pointed at a spindly representation
in the lower right-hand quadrant of the circle,
"with my granddaughter on my knee."

"Ah," I exhorted joyously, "so you can get out of the house!"
But my joy was premature.
He would not relinquish his sadness so easily,
certainly not for so casual a stranger as I.
"It was a long and difficult journey," he explained,
referring with a nod to the picture on the camera screen.
"I had to climb that mountain…"
"But you could have used the boat," I retorted,
caught up in his imagery.
"Look closer," he instructed with the patience of a true master
guiding the naive novice.

"The boat only has one oar!"
I was outmaneuvered and outgunned.
It would take a more skillful adversary than I
to break through his self-perpetuating solitude.

The evening continued pleasantly enough,
each poet in turn rendering his soul
through a prismatic filter of verbal construct.
Then the aged peaked cap and weathered nose
took his place behind the microphone
in the illuminated center of that light-starved room
and I waited with bated breath.
"I am A Lonely Man…" he began.

TO TOUCH A WHISPER

I grope in the dark,
touch a whisper.
What does it say?
Is it lonely like me,
disembodied, devoid of meaning and emotion?

Is it a lover's vow,
now lost in the emptiness of separation?
Will its memory fade,
washed away by tears of disappointment?
Or will it transmute and grow,
mocking, sneering at the naivety that succored it?

If I hold it to my bosom,
calm it, comfort it,
will it remember from whence it came?
Will it show me the way back
to its nigh forgotten nest
that I may warm my heart
in the dying embers of forgotten dreams?

WEEPING WILLOW

Weeping willow shed a leaf for me,
for all that was and could not be.
In oily dark reflection wrought,
fate-dashed dreams, mayfly-flit thought.
Bow'ed bough with slender fingers
forlorn and wind-brushed lingers
over ever-flowing water,
silent tears for son and daughter,
child of man striving to grow
in self-inflicted willful woe.
The river flows while time allows,
so too the tree with knarl'ed boughs
will shed its tears for you and me
and for all our dreams that could not be.

PHILOSOPHICAL

A BEGGAR AT THE TRAFFIC LIGHTS

I saw her from afar
as I approached the lights.
I prayed they'd stay green just long enough
to allow my conscience to sail through.

I wound up my window
as I was compelled to stop
by that inanimate intelligence that controls
the ebb and flow of our motorized existence.

I had long ago convinced myself
that such as she had wads of grimy bills
stuffed into her filthy mattress.
Had she no shame,
preying on the noble denizens of life's highway?

What right had she
to make me feel bad?
Was I not a worthy member of meritocracy?

She was neither young nor old.
Not ugly,
perhaps even attractive
beneath the shabby, dirt-shaded façade
that she wore like a uniform.

She thrust a crumpled plastic cup at the anonymous windows
as she passed down the line of metal cows.
Few were they that suckled her
with their pity.

She moved with dignity if not grace,
her face impassive.
They were not giving her charity.
She was the High Priestess of life's byways.
By accepting their pittance she absolved them of their guilt.

As she approached I wound down my window
a fraction and scrabbled for my wallet.
Like a bird trying to peck at a morsel
just out of reach beyond the bars of its cage,
she tried to thrust that well-used plastic cup
through the all-too-narrow space I had allowed.
She had touched my soul,
but I would not let her touch my body.

The lights will soon be changing,
I must make haste
if I'm to earn my salvation.

I wind the window down further
and the receptacle of her benevolence
is thrust through the widened gap.
My coins tinkle on top of others more veteran than they
and, before my mind has grasped what my heart has compelled,
the cup is withdrawn.

Coitus interruptus.
There was no act of love.
Neither foreplay nor final caress.
It was a business transaction.
You get what you pay for.

But for me it was a bargain.
No matter the wad of grimy bills
stuffed into an imaginary filthy mattress.
I did it for me, not for her.

And as I gently eased my steely steed
past the emerald green of life's onward flow
I blessed her
for allowing me to like myself
just that little bit more.

A LOOK IN THE MIRROR

I looked in the mirror
and what did I see?
A little boy with graz'ed knee
staring hopefully back at me.

I looked again and there I am,
a young and oh so angry man.
But stood I still while others ran?
No, I ran as they
and said I'd fight another day.

The mirror on the wall still hangs
and still I hear of hunger pangs
from Africa while
in Asia thousands die in storms
and First World greed exceeds all norms.

Still I look in the mirror,
and what do I see?
Not just this oh so haggard face
staring back in fallen grace,
but a little boy with graz'ed knee
whose accusing finger points at me.

A NIGHTMARE LAID TO REST

Last night I slept a sleep forlorn.
In dreams I saw a spirit form.
Its eyes were hidden by a shroud,
with whispered words on breath most fouled.

"I'm but a shadow in a land of mist.
Come! here's my blessing, my wraith-frost kiss!
You've dallied long in the world of men.
I miss your soul, come home again."

No, no, I cried, I know your face
you tempter of the human race.
I shun your sickly grin, your cold embrace.
Original sin's your nature base!

It made to grab my sweat-soiled hair.
Its hand outstretched to flesh laid bare.
From under filthy rags fossil-fingers stretched
and with yellowed nail in blood it etched.

"You are mine!" in crimson wrote,
its stark, cold fingers at my throat.
I fought my fear, no I'd not quit,
though strength-depleted, lacking wit.

In vain I struggled, gasped for air.
My life's thread hung on seconds spare.
As life and dream both twirled in space
each one in turn the other chased.

But lo! I saw a rosy light
that pierced the black eternal night.
And through my lids I did perceive
the Hand of Hope in heaven's sleeve.

At dawn the rays of newborn light
drove the demon from dream's sight
and I awoke reborn, anew,
not bathed in fear but morning dew.

A PALETTE REVOLUTION

Swathes of luminescent orange
cascade into cool pools of cucumber green,
each religiously preserving its own identity,
carving its own destiny in the chalk gray board.
Suddenly, right of center, a rich bugle sound,
resonating chords summoning a horde of violet Hussars
imperiously cutting a way through a throng of surly yellow.

But where are the whites?
Have they held back, aloof and disdainful,
worried that their purity be sullied
in the common multicolored struggle?
And the blues royal, have the milling crowds of hackneyed brown
cast them unceremoniously into those cavernous seas
of violent crimson?
The end is nigh and it is dressed in fathomless black,
devouring without trace or memory
the riotous colors that had fought so valiantly
for expression.

AN UNCOMMON PRAYER

When you pray to your god
what do you see?
A woman or a man is he?
And do you see him with a crown
on hair that's blond or wavy brown?
Is he different to you or me
depending on what we want to see?
For one without substance, it is clear,
needs corporeal embellishments to appear.

When you pray to your god
what do you ask?
Is it a selfish plea that him you task?
To win a game or profit by dare,
improve your lot, get a bigger share?
And will his judgment be less grim
if you succeed in flattering him?
Surely He does not need your praise
to sway Him in His heavenly ways.

And when you hurt your fellow man,
cheat and trip as best you can,
does God forgive you just the same
because you did it in His Name?
Is He so dependent on you
to pick His fights and win them too?
Is He your Champion, Majestic on High,
that bids you spit in your brother's eye?

Or, when you do imagine Him,
do you hear Him say, "Tear limb from limb!" ?
Do you believe He gave you the right
to be the cause of another's plight?
And when you have sealed humanity's fate
will God reward you for your hate?
An imagined heaven for those who make hell,
a reward for tolling another's bell.

(contd.)

(contd.)

Or will your destiny be elsewhere found,
buried in unhallowed ground?
Oblivion for all ill-gotten gains,
dust dispersed before almighty rains.
It is better to live in brotherly love
than try to flatter Him above.
Help raise the poor and the down-trod,
aid your neighbor, don't try to bribe God.

He needs not empty words of praise.
Let deeds not speech enrich your days.
And when your allotted span is through
you'll join the many and leave the few.
For all must loose their earthly ties
when their spirit onward flies.
Behind is left but a memory
of what we were and could not be.
What we did and did not do,
of pain we caused and laughter too.

APPEARANCES MISLEAD

You see the smile and laughing eyes,
but do you feel the pain and hear the sighs?
And one who dresses like a lord
not always wears what he can afford.
We try so dearly to impress,
to dignify a form burlesque.
Inner beauty toils in vain
to satisfy when lovers feign
to prefer kindness and a heart that's chaste
over lusty body and comely face.
They care not who we really are,
nor if the truth be near or far
from what we appear to be.
For their truth is only what they see.

CHOICES

If I could reel back hook and bait
and cast again in the river of fate,
would I choose that self-same bank
where I once sat before?

Or if I a pregnant turtle were
heavy with eggs one moonlit night
and I could choose,
would I crawl that self-same sandy shore?

As we tread life's twisted paths
at first our step is light and fast
and only impulse of reason bereft
points our compass right or left.
But as the shadows longer creep
we hesitate and tend to keep
to tracks we've trod before.

Even so, whether fast or slow,
inevitable end will seek us out.
No matter how long it takes,
with progress measured by mistakes,
we'll pass that time-locked door.

But when I look 'pon errors made,
each bore a child and some were fair.
And when I reflect on good deeds done
did starlight shine from every one?
If I could choose another path,
and thus those errors I'd not make,
would I deny those children fair
in errant hope that I could shine
more starlight in my wake?

But the Lord of Fate is kind.
For once beyond the end of time
decision and choice are left behind.
And it comforts me as the pace grows slow
that what is left is what I know
not what I could have done.
No more regrets, no salty wet,
no thoughts on a distant shore.
For what I would have done, I know,
is that which I did before.

DIVINE REWARD AND PUNISHMENT?

Are we naught but pets
kept in a cage,
rewarded for tricks
or punished in rage?

Are we just puppets
that dance on a string,
when our mouths are pulled open
we're prompted to sing?

Is every action ordained,
fixed from "above"?
Are we shunned for our sins
and blessed for our love?

We crave intervention
from a being divine,
pray for well-being,
look for a sign.

And what of The Craftsman
who made us all so?
Are we expected to guess
what he wants us to know?

Are we supposed to struggle
as best as we can
to try to decipher
His heavenly plan?

Has he made plain to us
exactly what's needed,
what is forbidden
and what must be heeded?

Are we all able,
are none born too weak,
are we all treated equal
both the strong and the meek?

But perhaps we're competing
each one on his own,
each reaping the wheat
that he himself's grown?

And what of those others
with no wheat to grow?
Will their seed be replenished
for another chance throw?

But why does He need us,
we're so imperfectly wrought?
And is it our doing
we're not born without fault?

Surely The Master,
The Ultimate Designer,
could fashion a creature
with judgment that's finer?

And what of the discord
between right versus wrong?
Is the Creator of Music
at odds with His song?

If we accept that
all that was made
was created by One
without any aid.

Then each thing was made perfect,
pure with intent,
no discord or struggle,
no wrong to lament.

(contd.)

(contd.)

And we are not needed,
not sent into the fray
to protect His honor,
for evil to slay.

When we were fashioned
in the esoteric "above"
we were made in His Image
in compassion and love.

And in love given freedom
in deed and in thought.
For without it what purpose
can in existence be sought?

But freewill comes not cheaply,
its price must be paid.
Mistakes lead to disasters,
often fate is man-made.

So we beg intervention,
we seek His control.
But in losing our freedom
we forfeit our soul.

In His wisdom and love
He heeds not our plea.
In His bounty He grants us
the gift to be free.

DON QUIXOTE'S LEGACY

So many windmills,
so little time.
So much is comic,
so little sublime.
O Quixote!
Where were you
when the words of so many
subdued those of so few?

O Spaniard
on faithful steed!
To us befalls
in time of need
to struggle
for a noble deed.
And though fun
they'll at us poke
it will not prevent
us honest folk
from speaking out
what must be spoke!

I AM MY BROTHER'S KEEPER!

Isn't private enterprise great!
You can make your fortune
out of another's fate.
Education, prisons, health
can all be converted into wealth.
Just buy a few shares in a company
and make some gold out of misery.
The state doesn't have to worry
about basic care,
nor about equal rights,
not about what's fair.
Just privatize on the trading floor.
Put some in but take out more.

But if private companies can make it work
why do governments their duties shirk?
They treat their citizens like homeless whores
but send them off to foreign wars.
Why shouldn't education be free
not just for parents with a company?
Being rich will always grant more power
for building your very own ivory tower.
Same with health and hospital beds.
If you've got more bucks you get better meds.
But is it fair that this should be?
Shouldn't good health care be given free?
Yes, if you're rich you can hire
a television in your private room
and get your bitter syrup
served on a silver spoon.
But the right of treatment for your pain
that should always be the same.

In law, why should the rich
buy a better defense?
Does poor equal guilty,
does that make sense?
If now social justice depends on gold
I wonder what future we'll behold.

Perhaps private armies
waging profitable wars?
Men being killed while the profit soars.
Or what about a force of private police,
to keep only the most gilt-edged peace?
No, as citizens of a state
it is only we who should decide our fate.
And if we want it to be fair,
sit Justice, not Profit, in the leader's chair.

LETTER TO A CHRYSALIS

A caterpillar have you been most of your life,
munching your way through leaf after boring leaf
of existential necessity.
You have crawled from one used, decaying framework to another,
gorging on what you found and moving on
when there was nothing more to be scavenged.

Your life has been spent inflating a material existence,
forever the same in essence,
just requiring more substance to fill an ever expanding presence,
as if size was the measure of your success.
But increased size only drives a more voracious appetite.
Veni, vidi, edi!
You came, you saw, you devoured.

But now, when it seems that this endless cycle of repetitive,
self-indulgent incorporation
must eventually engulf existence itself,
the season of your life is changing.
The sweet green leaves of summer
are now the dried decay of fall.

But you care not!
You have accumulated such girth
as to enable you to subsist on what you have become.
Your very weight has made you sluggish of change.
It has made you indolent to the world about you
and even your vast appetite has lapsed into lethargy.

Soon those brittle browns of autumn
will become the bare twigs of your emotional winter,
and you will insulate yourself from the cold
with layer upon layer of indifferent isolation.
Using your cloak of apathy
you rely on your material self-sufficiency
to weather the winter chill of lonely adversity.
You will lie dormant while the rays of an impartial sun
glance off a shunned earth.

But then, when Sol will warm to his perennial duty,
your self-awareness can split the binding restrictions of a past
existence.
Wings you had never dreamed of possessing
will expand in radiant, shimmering beauty.
You can attain heights of awareness that had always seemed
beyond reach.
When you emerge from your cocoon
your iridescent wings will radiate purity and love.
To be beauty is to act in beauty, not as a fleeting material persona,
but as a transcendental essence.
You can become that butterfly whose life is so short
but whose image continues to inspire long after its passing.
Imago, awake!

NATURE

I am the evening breeze,
the beat of a moth's wing.
You see me in the smile of babes,
the song that thrushes sing.

I am the lapping waves
that flirt with shingled shore,
the gossamer borne on the wind
that sighs for evermore.

You hear me in the silence
of the calm before a storm,
the patter of the raindrops
as I subtly change my form.

For I am gentle beauty,
the face of Nature mild.
But beware my pent-up anger
if my body be defiled!

For those that mistake meekness
for impotence be warned!
My anger knows no limits
when my portents are thus scorned.

The gentle breeze that brushed your cheek
will grow into a gale.
The lapping waves you thought so quaint
your puny dykes assail.

If you would have me keep my face
of kindness turned to you
then you must give me the respect
of which I know I'm due.

I am the beauty of your days,
your haven in the night.
Enjoy my bounty and be blessed
by Nature's kindly light.

OLD AGE

Like cobwebs on my face
the sultry years have passed,
in hastened stealth
they stole the wealth
of youth's exuberantly playful ploys
and preyed upon those mid-life joys
that compromise sound health.

As graying strands
in wispy bands,
hint of bygone thunder,
gaps in once pearly straight rows attest
to the impending absence of the rest
of this pirate's hoarded plunder.

O grant me the patience
of those so dear,
bright of eye, tender of year,
who need oftentimes repeat,
and with quiet understanding deference treat
an older, harder ear.

For I, in truth, cannot admit
that I, when of a younger wit,
did so serve in times of yore
those more senior in prime
who, with faltering steps like mine,
have trod these paths before.

PROBLEMS WITH THE NEIGHBORS

We're the oldest tenants on the block,
though some would disavow and mock.
They say our tenancy's just in name,
and that we have no prior claim.
The apartment's repainted, it's true,
the dusty browns now a brighter hue,
and few old features still remain
to prove the point that it is the same.

But the deeds are on record, none can deny,
though some still dispute it and call it a lie.
Indeed, we've been evicted before,
dragged kicking and screaming out the front door.
Our history of oppression you've probably read,
but those landlords are gone, disappeared, dead.
Cases of violence against us aren't rare,
with relatives murdered, children in despair.

And what have we done to deserve all this hate?
This universal attempt to annihilate?
It's all because of a family split.
A well-meaning son who wrote holy writ.
He was caught by the police, or so they say,
and punished severely for refusing to obey.
And we suffer those consequences for evermore
though we didn't do it and it wasn't our law!

There's also trouble with the Residents' Committee.
They say we've no right to be in this city.
The price of heating oil's tripled ever since we came.
The other tenants opine that we are to blame.
Their only solution to put everything right
is to pack up and clear out of everyone's sight.
Their Final Solution, which all debts would clear,
is to jump from the balcony and disappear!

TERRORISM

Fanatics fomenting religious strife,
terrorists destroying norms,
all those who without qualm harvest life
as if stalks of wheat before winter storms.

I've tried to understand their mind,
to get inside their complex head,
though often the thought I may succeed
fills me with fear and mortal dread.

For, to really understand what moves
another's thoughts and action
is to make reasonable what otherwise proves
a senselessly cruel distraction.

To deny shared destiny of mankind
results in alienation.
Man's self-centered, narrow mind
rejects universal integration.

Is it simply an immature ploy
to boost a tarnished, deformed heart?
For it's harder to build than to destroy,
give birth than tear a life apart.

If only we could respect our brother's view,
his thoughts cajole, try to persuade,
physical and mental harm eschew,
goodwill not creed-driven death parade.

THE CANVAS OF MY LIFE

In deeds I paint the canvas of my life,
brushstrokes of joy, desire and strife.
Thalo blue when I'm sad,
cadmium red when I'm feeling mad,
sienna browns from the earth in summer's furnace burn
and which will me embrace in turn.

In phrases I mix hues of emotions,
the ebb and flow of sin-capped oceans,
softly speak of citron love,
viridian below, cerulean above,
fluffy titanium white borne on gusts of hope,
the metal gray of brows that mope.

Thus, with my artistry complete
I my Maker prepare to meet,
to reveal the composition made,
some corners bent, some edges frayed.
and offer my work for Him to view
and prepare my soul refreshed, anew.

THOUGHTS ABOUT MATERIALISM

Discarded foil of chocolate ate,
Rorschach stains on an old beer mat,
empty bottles and vacant cans,
last years fashions and faded tans,
fabric of life grown thin and torn,
yesterday's best becomes tomorrow's worn,
last Sylvester's resolution broken,
what once was an emblem is now become a token.

And so the entropy of disorder grows,
the son must reap what the father sows,
only time grinds relentlessly on,
we want, we love, and tomorrow are gone.
Yet, like graffiti on life's wall,
we leave our mark, be it ever a scrawl,
a deed remembered, a smile, a tear,
that from afar can draw hearts near.

A child's delight so honest and free,
a majestic mountain or romantic sea,
wispy clouds chased in cerulean bliss,
lovers enjoying a half-blushed kiss,
newly-opened petals or tree bearing fruit,
the time to pause and in pausing moot
on all those things of honest worth,
free to enjoy on this bountiful earth.

THOUGHTS OF A HUMANIST

Let me wipe your tears
and salve your anguish
- if only for a moment.
Rest your troubled head on my shoulder
and I will bear your burden
- if only in part.
I ask only to bask
in the radiant warmth of your smile
- if only fleetingly,
and hear the echo of the thoughts
you choose to share with me
- if only in anonymity.
For in you I see my diminished reflection,
Your unseen eyes refresh my soul
- from now until the end of time.

THOUGHTS ON LIFE ETERNAL

Life Eternal! What will I be?
A youth, a parent, an older me?
And what special memories will I share?
Of those I've hurt beyond repair?
Or will I be a spirit free?
No hopes or thrills, a sexless me?
For what is the buzz and joy of life
if gained without toil, sweat and strife?

And if that being that once was me
remembers not how I used to be,
feels not the pain and joy in giving birth,
has no desire or sense of mirth,
will I know him, will I want to be
in such a life for eternity?
Or am I destined for ever to be
myself, a thought, a memory...?

Or will I aspire to spheres beyond
my material and earthly bond?
To reach the Throne of Heavenly Might,
to bathe in joy of Creation's Light
and merge at last, infinite delight!
with all the love of truth and right,
to be lost and found in spiritual bliss,
is anything more sublime than this?

THREE BLIND MEN IN A DARK ROOM

Imagine, you are a blind man in a dark room.
What is "blind" if you have never known "vision",
yet alone been aware of someone else
who has experienced sight?

And why does the room have to be dark
if you have no awareness of vision?
It does not have to be, it just is.
Situations exist without being dependent on us.
There *can* be a sound of a tree falling even though
there is no one around to hear it.

What is a room?
It is a bounded space in which you exist.
You can feel the boundaries
but cannot know what is outside them.
Is there anything outside them?

And what does it mean to "feel" them?
You are relying on your senses.
But can you rely on them?
Are they fed by reliable information?
Is your interpretation correct?
You assume so because
without external information
you can draw no conclusions
about the world outside of you.
But how do you know there is a world outside of you?
You assume so because of your senses –
but that is a circular, self-contained argument.

There are two other blind men in the room with you.
How do you know?
They have told you so.
They have told you they are blind.
Again, what is blind?
Since not one of you has experience of vision
none can even think of being blind,
yet alone define it.

And how can you be sure that they are really there?
You hear their voices,
you feel their bodies.
You assume that what you hear and feel is reliable information.
You assume.

Our most basic understanding of ourselves and our world
is based on assumption.
Is there nothing that is independently and inherently true?
Mathematics! Is that not consistent and true?
One plus one is two.
The most fundamental statement in mathematics
on which everything else is built.
It states that if I have a certain defined object
and then have another object identical in every way
to the first, then, I can label the entity of both as "two".
It is true only if I can assume they are identical.

But numbers are symbols to be manipulated
independently of the world we sense.
Even in this abstract, self-contained world of mathematics
is "one" plus "one" always "two"?
If I have one "nothing" and another "nothing"
I still have only "one" nothing.
If I have one "infinity" and another "infinity" I will,
when they are combined, still only have
"one" infinity.
So mathematics is only true if we so define it to be
according to the rules we lay down.

And so you remain, blind.
One of three men, you assume,
all blind, apparently,
in what you call a room,
for want of a better expression.

(contd.)

(contd.)

You cannot really know for certain
anything about yourself,
yet alone anything about what you feel
is external to yourself.

Yet you have awareness.
You cannot know if your senses are reliable.
In fact, sometimes the information you receive
from some senses
conflicts with information received from others.
But you are aware of them.
So you define your existence by your awareness.

When you cease to be aware you will cease to exist,
as defined by yourself.
It will be a state of unconsciousness,
either temporary or permanent.

And your awareness has a property called curiosity.
It is what drives you to explore your dark room
and your other companions
whom your senses tell you are here together with you.

It is your curiosity that drives you
to speculate on the existence of a space
outside the boundaries of your room
and the nature of whatever "light"
may exist beyond these walls,
beyond the three blind men in a dark room.

TO YOU, TESTOSTERONE!

Testosterone! I am a Man.
I raise a gilded chalice to Your Name,
Oh Driver of My Destiny!
Inflator of My Ego!

For you I will rape and pillage.
In your name will I subjugate my enemies,
be it on the battlefield or in the boardroom,
on the playing field or in a lover's bed.
I will be supreme!

You raised me from a suckling babe
and taught me how to rant and rave
for other kiddies' toys.
And in your name I do it still,
Yay, even though I'm old and gray,
I do it still.

Yet be not fooled
by my acquiescence to your will.
It is out of weakness that I obey you.
For I know within my heart of hearts
that you care not for me.
"Survival of the Fittest!"
That is the motto inscribed upon your crest.

And in my most private soul,
within the tender petals that me enfold,
still dwells that little boy,
so vulnerable, so shy,
who would caress with gentle touch
and be caressed in turn.

(contd.)

(contd.)

But You, oh mighty mover of my biochemistry,
have strengthened the fortress walls of my being.
Only the obstinate few can pass over the drawbridge
to the inner keep.
And I too am locked within.
Unable to communicate with those who wait outside,
and oft must turn away.

And when you are done with me
will you cast me aside like a used condom?
Will I with soft regret and tearful eye
review my subservience to your will?
When I am old and toothless will I serve you still
even though I have no bite?
Will my pride still be fed by you?
Or will your hold on me thin,
as surely as the thinning hairs on my balding head?
Will the words "I'm sorry, I was wrong" break through?
For even now they almost do …

WHAT IS ART?

Crafted rhymes, constructed meter,
forcing words like "saltpeter"
into a context obscure?
Or a room in a gallery
containing only shredded newspaper
or cow manure?

The shock effect.
Is that art?
Calling a poem "I don't give a fart!"?
Or a dissected horse,
does that fit the part?

Must it really be enigmatic,
a dynamic event shown strangely static?
Is craftsmanship art or just skilled design?
Can we really tell the gaseous pop
from the full-bodied wine?

For me art is intriguing use of a symbol's refrain
to tap into our emotional plane,
to strike a common chord in resonance complete
with the artist's view, its beat
an echo of his mind.

To glimpse, to touch, to feel
the essence of his thoughts unreel
and, whether willingly or in protest,
lead us inexorably on
to what his heart now dwells upon.
To marvel not just at his technique
but at his very soul to peek.

WOMAN, SPEAK!

I blame you...
for all those young men
that in wars die.
For want of your voice they lie
in forgotten fields.
Brothers, fathers, sons of men
whom you can never love again.

You gave them joy of life, and milk,
clothed in caresses of soft spun silk.
But did your mother's voice complain
when they were marched off in your name?
Where was your matronly staying hand
when they proudly strutted with martial band
and trumpet notes that rent the air?
O tell me, Woman, were you not there?

You claim to be the weaker race,
and yet I see in your birth-creased face
that more suffering can you bear
than a thousand virile men could share.
And yet your voice is strangely meek.
O Woman, I beg you, speak!

WORLD PEACE NOT PIECES

Crumpled sheets in the waste-bin
of human affairs.
Official versions
not everyone shares.
Did it really occur or was it invented?
Can we on history rely
to separate truth
from convincing lie?

And millions die.

Does it matter
what really occurred?
Do you think it plausible
or simply absurd?
Whether a fact be false or true
often depends on your point of view.
A personal story carries the weight
of someone's love or another's hate.
But what of legends old
tales of vengeance and loyalty sold?
Racial memories of events blighted
by being told and retold,
with passions re-ignited,
its history confirmed by being recited?

And thus millions die.

So much hate and national strife
pervade our personal everyday life
because of collective remembered sins,
each drawn from history's rubbish bins.
So how can global friction end?
We need statesmen not politicians
for wounds to mend.

(contd.)

(contd.)

The only way for peace to grow
is by accepting a status quo.
Not of injustice for the weak
but in triumph of the meek.
A victory of conscience and love
over dissension and blood-stained dove.

So that millions will not die.

Is this too ideal for you?
Do you think the jackals
would not allow you to?
True, opportunists would not be slow
to make their very own status quo!
Only a union of determined states
could impose peace on rival hates
and make them swallow a bitter pill
to implement enforced goodwill.
An organization like this exists,
though these objectives have oft been missed.
But it's the only hope we have.

To save millions who will die.

It must gird its loins and intercede
wherever good sense perceives the need.
East Timor, Sri Lanka and, not least,
Darfur as well as The Middle East.
Kashmir, Taiwan and The West Bank,
an international army to pull rank.
Immediate cessation of violence,
a multinational fence,
a unified force of common sense,
to prevent man's historic desire
to incinerate in self-ignited fire.

And if not, millions will die.

WHIMSICAL

COURTSHIP

(Says he…)
Gentle m'am, forgive my stare.
Your soft brown eyes,
your coiffured hair
are more than mortal man can bear.

Sweet Fantasy of heaven born,
to see your smile
with such poise worn
drives slumber from my eyes forlorn.

And if you think my honeyed tongue
is naught but praise
in bad taste sung
then I, your servant, should be hung.

But so pure and perfect such as thee
need have no fear
of such as me
who a Gentleman would always be.

(She replies…)
In truth, Dear Sir, you are too bold.
Your eyes look deep,
though my hair, I'm told,
is indeed wondrous to behold.

Your praise, 'tis true, so soothes my ear.
As to your reasons,
yea, these I fear,
so please refrain from standing near!

And if you think my reaction cold
be not put off
by words that scold.
Ladies dare not quickly fold.

For such as I a man must woo.
A patient man,
a man like you,
will surely know just what to do…

EGO AND SUPERFICIALITY

"I'm the best!" said Ego.

"You'd never think so to look at you," Superficiality replied.

"You can talk! All you think about is your appearance!"
retorted Ego.

"It's looks that count!" Superficiality reposted.

"Do you really believe that anyone actually cares what you
think as long as you look good?" she continued.

Ego was almost crushed by Superficiality's view were it not
for Virtue's intervention.

"Let's compromise," said the latter.

"You both compliment each other.

For what is Ego without Superficiality,
and how can Superficiality survive without Ego?"

And what of Virtue?

To keep from being crowded out of existence
she would do well to distance herself from both Ego
and Superficiality!

I PREFER BRAND X

They say that I am stupid
and that I have no brain.
They wonder why I'm not locked up
for being quite insane.

They showed it on the TV,
 laundry before and after,
 and said they could not understand
 why this should cause such laughter.

But Brand X is so much cheaper
and my washing looks the same,
so why pay so much dearer
just 'cause it has a name?

The bank asked me for my money.
They said I'd make a pile
if only I knew how to invest,
then one could live in style.

At first I thought he meant for me
a lifestyle for which I hanker.
But then I saw the life he meant
was meant for him the banker.

They told me to believe in Him
 'cause only the Priesthood knew
the secret of life eternal,
revealed to the Sacred Few.

But they were so divisive
and each secret so arcane.
Why should God entrust to them
the secret of His Name?

(contd.)

(contd.)

They dressed me in a uniform,
and sent me off to fight.
It was a sacred duty.
They said that might was right.

I saw men die and others hurt.
Peace finally was attained.
But it was only for the rich
and some others that remained.

They say that I am stupid.
Maybe I cry in vain.
They think I should be put away.
D'you think that I'm insane?

I TOLD YOU SO!

O what satisfaction springs,
such boundless joy it brings,
when you say, "I told you so!"
while your self-confidence in contrast soars,
the stream of smugness that from it pours
washes all empathy away.

"I told you so!"
Said with alchemistic scorn
that friend turns into foe.
A phrase of blameless self-righteousness born
that seeds of enmity will sow.

For all that hear it really know
that no one sees what's out of sight,
and there's not a man who's always right.
So heed these words before you go
and remember always,
I told you so!

LIFE'S SO UNFAIR!

Life's so unfair!
"Come on, O Great Almighty", he said,
"Why don't you strike *me* down instead?!"
Next day,
"Death By Spontaneous Combustion"
It read.

ODE TO A DISSATISFIED WIFE

Your expectations of me,
in truth, are not fair.
In your silence I hear you,
am shrunk by your stare.

Would you then have me
go down on my knees?
Would you respect me
if I did what you please?

Though you claim with some reason
that I am too hard,
at times when I'm softer
your pleasure is marred.

If I were a puppet
to dance on your string
would that make you happy
and make your heart sing?

ODE TO A HEN-PECKED HUSBAND

Fear not the frenzied, gnashing jaws.
Do not retreat from those saber-tipped claws.
For she will smell the stink of your sweat.
If you run she'll attack, on that you can bet!
The only recourse if you want to survive
 is wash up the dishes, keep the marriage alive!

ODE TO SMS

If all the C's
could be swum with E's
and all the J's
@ all the B's,
then would the alphabet
stop its T's?

If asked Y
we had 2 Q so L8
2 drink the T,
so X L N-tly made by U,
just say it was our F8.

Y U R O'd
nobody knows.
I suppose it's in UR P-green I's
this conundrum of letters lies :)

PEOPLE ARE LIKE ONIONS

With black-brown skin, pale, red or yellow,
pungent smell, or one more mellow,
layer upon layer like deceit,
one to flatter, one to cheat.
Flesh that panders to every taste,
those that lust, others chaste.
Nourishing sin with sprouting fingers,
iniquity, fetid, on breath lingers.
Others, fearful of their fate,
pray with fervor, their end await,
whether in rings to be sliced
or thrown in boiling oil when diced.

SONG OF THE TROUBADOUR

A wandering troubadour am I,
the hearts of maidens fair I cheer,
and if their lord is not nearby
they oft times join me for a beer.

Our country beer is warm but flat,
so too our maidens, without a doubt.
But a pint's a pint, I'll drink to that!
Best not to thirst than go without.

And so it was one summer's day,
when errant knights in joust compete,
that I took refuge in some hay
to comfort our squire's mistress sweet.

For poor young thing she was distraught
that her betrothed, for wont of skill,
a manikin of straw had bought
with which to practice his sword drill.

No sooner was my lyre took out,
her musical ear for to enchant,
came from a distance such a shout
sent lyre and maiden all aslant!

Forsooth an artist such as I
abides no such discordant note,
and fearing for my lyre – Goodbye!
I hastened deftly to the moat.

By this time the bridge was down,
I passed my lord on his way in.
My hot flushed face, his withering frown
seemed to hint at carnal sin.

A wandering troubadour am I,
sometimes my music grates on ears.
I must admit for I cannot lie,
my playing oft results in tears.

THE BEAST

The Beast appears out of pure thin air,
one moment normalcy, the next he is there.
You never invite him in,
never know whence he came.
But after his arrival nothing's the same.

He's called The Beast 'cause he's far from tame.
With his bloodshot look and his unkempt mane
you can tell that he's wild.
At first you think that you'll die
from fear of his power,
from his piercing red eye.

But then, in a moment of reckless intent
you jump up on his back without asking consent.
Ride him 'till you drop!
Maybe his bucking will have you unseated,
but try to stay on.
An adventure like this is seldom repeated.

At first he'll wake you just before dawn.
Bleary-eyed yawning you'll get jabbed by his horn.
You simply have no choice but to comply.
If you stay in your bed and to get up refuse,
he'll leave you forever, dazed and bemused.

Oftentimes he'll steal up on you,
attack from behind.
Suddenly, mid-conversation, he'll play with your mind.
"Is he eccentric, confused?"
Friends who have known you for years
will talk of your strangeness and express morbid fears.

But when you get used to him
you'll frankly admit,
without him you'd feel trapped in a bottomless pit.
He'll become the tool of your deepest expression.
You'll no longer fear that his nature's not tame,
for The Beast that you ride, Creativity his name!

SO, YOU WANT TO FALL IN LOVE?

OK, so you're complaining that love
is eluding you?
You don't know how lucky you are!
Enjoy sex, it's great.
But, at all cost, AVOID LOVE!

Love is a parasite.
It'll invade your body and your mind,
nay, your very soul, and take over.
The normal, hard-working, well-balanced adult
that everyone knows and respects
will now be transformed, quicker than it takes
to find the center-fold bunny in Playboy,
into a manic-depressive, "danger-to-himself-and-others",
irresponsible teenager.

The guy the company trusts to invest
millions of dollars for its pension fund
will be found, at 3 in the morning,
hanging over an interstate trying to paint
"Stevie loves Lora" on the bridge
Lora passes under on her way to work.

And the marvel of it is
that this alchemistic transmutation
from blue steel to "fool's gold"
only requires a few molecules of pheromone.

Would anyone in his right mind
wish for lunacy like this?
Would you want to be the object of attention
of a lunatic like this?
To be bombarded with inane protestations of love,
sms's, flowers, chocolates...?
Yes, a kind word once in a while,
flowers on a weekend, chocolates on your birthday...
but bombarded!!?? Day after love-sodden day?

(contd.)

(contd.)

And if you're not quick enough to respond
to messages, to sms's...?
After all, the speed of light is limited to 300,000 km/sec...
Can you withstand those baleful, reproachful eyes,
that hangdog expression of inordinate hurt?

The only silver lining to this somber aspect
of the human condition
is that it doesn't last...
well, not for more than a few weeks,
months at most.

Unlike most insanities it is self-limiting,
although the way to recovery passes through
a mine-field of explosive emotions
that can leave you scarred for life.

So give me friendship,
give me sex,
give me the enjoyment of shared moments of pleasure,
but, PLEASE, keep me away from LOVE.

Oh, no...I feel it starting...sucking me...
down the rabbit-hole agaiiiiiiin...

TO YOU

Thank you for taking time to pause
away from all those other chores.
To dwell upon small buds I grew,
to nurture shoots as they peek through
the soil of my fertile thoughts.
By appreciating such poignant cadence
you disseminate its mild, fresh fragrance
and allow its petals to caress the dew.
In thanks this verse I wrote for you.

ANNOTATIONS

CHOICES

A somewhat difficult poem having an irregular meter that is, nevertheless, lilting in quality.

The theme is one of possible regret and undetermined, or even unexpected or uncalculated consequences of decisions made.

The allegorical turtle has been chosen as a symbol of an animal that always returns to the same place to lay her eggs.

The poem describes the course of a life from impulsive youth ("at first our step is light and fast" and "only impulse of reason bereft...") to the more experienced and balanced, even excessively careful, period of old age ("But as the shadows longer creep we hesitate and tend to keep to tracks we've trod before.").

But, whether we hasten or not, we will finally all reach the end of our life and pass on from our present temporal existence ("we'll pass that time-locked door").

The poem goes on to examine the consequences of supposed errors that have been made. Were they all negative? Not at all, sometimes errors can have positive outcomes ("each bore a child and some were fair"). Not only that, but sometimes a success can result in a negative outcome ("when I reflect on good deeds done did starlight shine from every one?").

This begs the question, if you could wind back "the film" would you correct those "errors" and also lose some of those positive consequences that resulted from them ("If I could choose another path...would I deny those children fair")?

In fact, the question is theoretical because there is no going back ("once beyond the end of time decision and choice are left behind"). Not only that, but there is little point in regret ("what is left is what I know not what I could have done"). Tears are pointless ("no salty wet").

The conclusion is that at the time we make decisions we can know little about their eventual outcome. Some were bad decisions that had good consequences and some were well-meant decisions that, nevertheless, had negative results and, all in all, we have to accept the bad with the good without regret ("For what I would have done, I know, is that which I did before").

DIVINE REWARD AND PUNISHMENT?

This is another poem that is written in a deceptively easy way and yet attempts to deal with complex philosophical issues by asking seemingly simple questions. The very fact that it was written at all expresses the poets view that it is the right of Man to question his Creator – an idea much promulgated in the Old Testament in the stories of Abraham, Moses etc.

The intention is to clarify ideas regarding our perception of a monotheistic deity.

The assumption made, of course, is that there is one Ultimate Force responsible for the creation of everything. Even if we were to assume a pantheon of supernatural beings, viz. gods, it is natural to assume that one of them would be superior to all the others for the reason of there being unity and harmony in the laws of the physical universe. In fact, from a historical perspective, pantheons of gods were invoked in the pre-scientific period before it was apparent that nature was in harmony.

The alternative to a belief in creation by One Intelligent Being is to believe that the universe/s always existed or are always being created spontaneously.

The first question asked by the poet is, are we just for the "amusement" of The Deity ("...rewarded for tricks...")?

Without answering, the questions continue. Are we just puppets ("...that dance on a string..."), is divine reward and punishment a sort of conditioning ("...shunned for our sins and blessed for our love...")?

It is because of these feelings of being a pet looked after by its owner that we ask The Deity for help ("We crave intervention ...pray for wellbeing, look for a sign").

But why do we have to second-guess, why does He not simply make His wishes plain and understood ("Are we expected to guess...to struggle...to decipher...")?

If we are expected to decipher, what of those who are not equipped with the intellect to do so ("...born too weak...")?

Does he treat us all the same ("...are we all treated equal...")?

The poet then proposes another idea. Are we each tested according to how we perform with the tools each has been given and not judged by the same standard each and all ("...perhaps we're competing each one on his own")?

Even in this idea there is an enormous problem. Some individuals do not have the intellect at all to think about their actions ("...what of those others with no wheat to grow?"). Do they get another chance in another life ("...another chance throw...")?

And what, indeed, is our purpose? Especially as we seem to have been created with so many imperfections. If we were created for a purpose could we not have been created more perfectly and uniformly ("...could fashion a creature with judgment that's finer...")?

The poet goes on to discuss the imperfections of the world, especially the apparent struggle between right and wrong. If the Deity created everything then did He also create "evil" ("Is the Creator of Music at odds with His song...")?

This would appear to be inconsistent with the idea of a perfect universe created by a Perfect Being. Such a perfect universe is also at odds with the Epicurean idea that The Deity created the universe and then left it to its own devices which need correcting. It is at this point that the poet attempts to enlighten us with his monotheistic world view ("...each thing was made perfect...pure with intent...no discord...no wrong to lament").

Not only that, but he also proposes that our role is not one of "sacred warriors" ("...we are not needed, not sent into the fray to protect His honor, for evil to slay...").

The very opposite, we were created in love. And, in love, given free choice.

This idea is opposed to the Newtonian vision of a mechanical universe where every outcome is calculable and therefore preordained. It is, in fact, supported by the Theory of Quantum Physics in which the "observer" changes the reality of any possible outcome.

For, as the poet argues, what is the point of thought, struggle, or life itself if we have no independent effect on the result ("...what purpose can in existence be sought...")?

But the result of freewill together with our independent nature frequently results in disaster ("...freewill comes not cheaply... often fate is man-made...").

It is then that we beg for intervention but, in doing so we are really asking to give up what makes us human ("...But in losing our freedom we forfeit our soul...").

The poet concludes that because of The Deity's love and understanding He will not let us forfeit our independence ("...In His bounty He grants us the gift to be free...").

The ideas represented here are in many ways similar, if viewed at a slightly different angle, of those expressed in the biblical Book of Job.

DON'T TELL ME THAT YOU LOVE ME

In this piece the subject addressed is the meaning and expression of love as apposed to declarations of love. The poet requests true love rather than beautiful but empty words. There is also an allusion to the true nature of love ("care", "to share"), even in the modern age of unrivalled ambition ("True love is not outdated though ambition takes the lead.").
Towards the end of the poem the gauntlet is really thrown down viz. "if you really mean it....make sure you're really there." i.e. no empty promises.
Finally, the poet declares that he would rather do without a love that is fickle, sometimes ignoring the other party and at other times expressing false feelings ("when to shun and when to pose").
The style starts off with quite a regular meter which is broken in the final stanza adding a rather melodious finale.

IN LOVE WITH THE WOMAN YOU WERE

In this piece the poet attempts to rationalize his changed feelings towards the once-object of his love. In addition, he expresses his yearning for that previous entity who he still claims to be in love with ("Yes, I am still in love with the woman I thought you were"). The change in viewpoint and accompanying change in emotion is likened to the change that takes place in the mind of an observer of an optical illusion ("...a drawn illusion compels my mind...").
The imagery of swans is used allegorically to signify the faithfulness and constancy of true love, as these aquatic birds pair for life.
But, although the poet expresses his disappointment in his love's apparent change ("...so cynically slew the swans..."), yet he also ponders his own culpability in not being aware of answering to his former love's possible cries for help. Was he insensitive? And was his insensitivity a contributing factor in the changed relations between them ("Did she cry for help within that shell? ...and was I deaf?")?

Or is he being too hard on himself ("Or is the illusion just in my mind?")?

His uncertainty results in his questioning of the original presence of the object of his emotions ("Or were you ever there at all...?").

Did she ever exist in the form that he perceived her, or did he invent her and imbue his erstwhile lover with a nature she never really had? Love is blind...

PROBLEMS WITH THE NEIGHBORS

The imagery alludes to the history of The Jewish People and the political situation in the Middle East.

This is a very difficult and emotive subject and, therefore, almost paradoxically, can be broached most effectively through the medium of verse.

There is no doubt that the Jews have the longest historical record of any people in the area ("the oldest tenants on the block") although in some quarters it is a matter of contention ("that we have no prior claim").

The modern history of The State of Israel can also appear, to some, to erroneously contradict a continuous Jewish presence in the area ("the apartment's repainted").

Nevertheless, the Bible, as accepted by the three monotheistic religions, is unequivocal in its support of Jewish claims to the Promised Land ("..the deeds are on record, none can deny"). This stanza also refers to the expulsion of the Jews from Israel ("dragged kicking and screaming...") both in 586 BCE (Babylonians under Nebuchadnezzar) and in 135 CE (by the Romans following the Bar Kochba revolt), although these expulsions were never complete and there always remained a continuous Jewish presence in the country. The poem goes on to allude to the Holocaust ("..relatives murdered, children in despair.") and attempts, briefly, to mention the root of antisemitism ("a family split...a son who wrote holy writ...punished severely...").

Notwithstanding, the poet ridicules the burden of guilt being placed so unjustly on the shoulders of all Jews, even those living 2000 years after the original event and the fact that the arrest and execution were carried out by Romans and according to Roman law ("...we didn't do it and it wasn't our law!").

Progressing to the 20th century mention is made of The Arab

League opposing Israel's right to exist ("the Resident's Committee... say we've no right to be in this city.") and the use of the "oil weapon" ("The price of heating oil's tripled").

Again, there is an allusion to the Final Solution of World War II. The apparent solution that would satisfy everyone else, the poet sarcastically concludes, is to commit national suicide.

THOUGHTS ON LIFE ETERNAL

The poem attempts to grapple with, or at least to bring into focus, "practical" aspects of "life after death".

Do we take on a form in the afterlife?

If so, do we appear as we did in earthly life ("A youth, a parent, an older me")?

Or all things to all observers?

Will we have complete recall of everything we did, even things we would prefer to forget ("...what special memories will I share? Of those I've hurt beyond repair...")?

Or will we be formless ("...a spirit free...")?

In either case what emotions or drives will we have, if at all ("No hopes or thrills, a sexless me...")? For, surely, there is pleasure in a corporeal existence and in the rough and tumble of earthly life ("For what is the buzz and joy of life if gained without toil, sweat and strife?").

The second stanza questions if we really want an afterlife if it is to be so different from our present one. Or, to put it another way, if we will be so different to how we are now will we in fact recognize ourselves ("will I know him...") and is this the eternal future we are waiting for ("...will I want to be in such a life for eternity?"). This stanza concludes with the idea that perhaps, after all, the best we can hope for is to live on as a cherished memory in the awareness of others ("...am I destined for ever to be myself, a thought, a memory...?").

The third stanza expresses the esoteric view of the union of souls in a spiritual utopia.

WHITE DOVE

The White Dove represents "pure love" in contrast to the lust
signified by the phoenix.

The poem has many sexual connotations and motifs viz. "moistened
sweetly by love's dew", "the thrust of passion's fire", "in embrace
to sow life's seed" and "intoxicating, musky scent envelops fields of
passions spent."

The first verse and final verses allude to the constant nature of
true love (in its asexual sense) soaring above the commonalities of
everyday life and the eternal struggles of all strata of society. This
contrasts with the inconstant, one might say fickle, nature of sexual
attraction and biological drive.

The term "contrasts" is used without any judgmental overtones.
Both sexual and asexual love have their place in the fabric of human
society, both are important and, indeed, complementary.